TOO-LATE TOBY
by TONY GARTH

Toby was late for everything.

Absolutely everything.

He was late getting up in the morning. And every day he was late for school.

It was always getting him into trouble.

Toby's supper was always cold because he never came when his Mum called. He was always the last to sit down at the table.

"Oh Toby," his Mum said. "Your supper's ruined. As usual."

He left everything to the last minute. Even going to the toilet. It could be very embarrassing.

"Oh Toby," said his teacher. "Not again."

Toby always arrived at parties after everyone else had left.

"Sorry, Toby," his friends said. "You missed a great party."

He was even too late for the snow in winter.

By the time he went sledging, it was spring.

He was very disappointed.

One night, as he lay in bed, Toby made his mind up. He was fed up with being late.

"From tomorrow, I'm going to be on time for everything," he said to himself. "Or even early."

He found four very large, very loud alarm clocks and set them for early next morning. Very early indeed.

Next morning at dawn, the clocks went off. Bzzzz! Bzzzz! Bzzzz! They made a dreadful din. It woke up Toby, and his parents, and their neighbours. They were not very happy at all.

Toby leapt out of bed. He'd slept in his school uniform. He thought it would save time.

Toby ran downstairs.

He was far too early for breakfast so he went outside to wait for the school bus.

The sun was just rising in the sky.

He waited and waited. But still the school bus didn't arrive.

"I must be too early," Toby thought.

He decided to run all the way to school instead.

It didn't take long to get to school. But when he got there, the gates were locked. And there was no one else in sight.

"I must be the first one here," he thought. "Everyone will be surprised."

Just then Toby's teacher jogged past in her tracksuit.

"Hello, Toby," she said. "What on earth are you doing at school today?"

"I'm being early," Toby replied.

"Two days early," his teacher said, smiling. "It's Saturday!"

Toby went home.

"Being early is much too tiring," he said, as he slumped in his chair. Just in time to miss his favourite show on TV.

Look out for the next twelve Little Monsters!

FRIENDLY FRANCO

CLUMSY CLARISSA

BOISTEROUS BILLY

SICKLY SIMON

SERIOUS SADIE

GROWN-UP GABBY

PERFECT PRUDENCE

RUDE ROGER

DANGEROUS DAVE

CURIOUS CALVIN

DIRTY DERMOT

TANTRUM TABITHA

© SPLASH! Holdings Ltd.

Cover printed Hexachrome, inner section printed 4 colour process by Speedprint (Leeds) Ltd. Tel: 0113 245 3665.